JUL 27 1999

00401578 8

P9-CSH-298

# Silver Rain Brown

*For Roseann Walsh,*
*whose teaching and encouragement*
*were rain to me*
*—M. C. H.*

*For Pablo*
*—T. F.*

Text copyright © 1999 by M. C. Helldorfer
Illustrations copyright © 1999 by Teresa Flavin

All rights reserved. For information about permission
to reproduce selections from this book, write to
Permissions, Houghton Mifflin Company, 215 Park Avenue South,
New York, New York 10003.

The text of this book is set in Frutiger
The illustrations are gouache on Canson Mi-Teintes paper

*Library of Congress Cataloging-in-Publication Data*

Helldorfer, Mary-Claire, 1954–
Silver Rain Brown / M. C. Helldorfer ; illustrated by Teresa Flavin.
p. cm.
Summary: One hot dry summer, a young boy and his mother wait
for the much-needed rain and for the birth of their new baby.
ISBN 0-395-73093-7
[1. Summer—Fiction. 2. Rain and rainfall—Fiction. 3. Babies—Fiction.]
I. Flavin, Teresa, ill. II. Title.
PZ7.H37418Si 1999
[E]—dc21 97-17738 CIP AC

Printed in Singapore
TWP 10 9 8 7 6 5 4 3 2 1

# Silver Rain Brown

**M. C. Helldorfer**    *Illustrated by* **Teresa Flavin**

Houghton Mifflin Company
Boston 1999

**Can't cool down.**
**No, we can't cool down.**

Momma's grown round as
the August moon, a fat gold balloon
rising over Sister Maria's neon sign:
FORTUNES TOLD HERE.
But who needs a crystal ball
to tell how hot we'll be tomorrow?

**Can't cool down.**
**No, we can't cool down—**
no rain this summer.
We can't wash cars,
can't water gardens.

Each morning's like the one before.
*What'll happen to my little flowers?*
Momma says, her arms around her big belly,
rock, rocking slow like she's
already holding the baby.

*Make us a breeze, Momma.*
**Can't cool down.**

Keisha comes around with all her sisters.
She stretches like a cat on our front steps.

*We're Egyptians,* Keisha says.
*And I'm Cleopatra.*
Now we got to fan her.

**Just can't cool down.**

Teddy's on the sidewalk
trying to fry an egg, believing
whatever his grandpa says—
he says it's hot enough to.

Keisha laughs at Teddy, and that gets him mad.
Tempers rise like red in a thermometer.
**Can't cool down!**
Digging down in Teddy's carton,
we come up throwing, and splatter
all those hot yellow suns.

*Scrambled eggs,* Momma sighs,
pulling me inside, shaking her head.
Sometimes she looks so serious,
worrying about her flowers again.

But we can't waste water,
can't water gardens, can't wash cars,
can't open the fire hydrants.

Four A.M. and I can't sleep,
wishing Daddy would come back,
wishing, wishing it would rain.

Momma gets up, fills cook pots with water.
We tiptoe out. We water all the little flowers
and Sister Maria's rosebush.
We water all the squares of brown grass
up and down the block.

Then we sleep through the hot day.

That night, it rains.

**Rains! Rains!**

Everybody runs out their doors.

RETA E. KING LIBRARY

We're fish, our wet skins shining,
our big fish mouths gulp-gulping
down the rain.
We're jungle explorers—

we run through a rain forest, crossing
bridges over rush-rushing streams.
We stand for a long time
under a waterfall.

My shoes sail away,
looking for a harbor.
I fish them out and paddle home.
Momma's watching me, not so serious now.
Smiling a little now.
*No bath tonight,* she says.
We shower under a streetlamp.

At midnight, it's raining still,
just soft silver rain.
We take a taxi through the silver rain,
Momma and I.
Our baby comes.

I want to call her Silver.
Momma wants to call her Rain.

Sister Maria cuts a rose,
predicting better times for us—

and Silver Rain Brown.